LADYBIRD BOOKS, INC.
Lewiston, Maine 04240 U.S.A.
© LADYBIRD BOOKS LTD MCMLXXXVII
Loughborough, Leicestershire, England

Printed in England

The Three
Billy Goats Gruff

Adapted by DONNA R. PARNELL
Illustrated by STEVE SMALLMAN

Ladybird Books

Once there were three billy goats named Gruff.

They lived near a meadow
of sweet green grass.

The three billy goats Gruff
wanted to eat the sweet green grass
that grew in the meadow.
But they had to cross a bridge
to get there.

An ugly troll lived under the bridge.
He gobbled up anyone
who tried to cross it.
So the three billy goats Gruff
stayed home.

One day, Little Billy Goat Gruff said,
"I will go to the meadow
to eat the sweet green grass.
I will cross the bridge."

Trip-trap, trip-trap,
went his feet on the bridge.

Out came the ugly troll.
"Who is that, trip-trapping
across my bridge?"
he roared.

"It is I, Little Billy Goat Gruff,"
said the goat.

"I am coming to gobble you up!"
said the troll.

"Oh, no," said Little Billy Goat Gruff.
"I am too small to eat.
Wait for my brother,
Middle Billy Goat Gruff.
He is fatter and tastier than I am."
"All right," said the troll.
"You may cross the bridge."

So Little Billy Goat Gruff
went into the meadow,
to eat the sweet green grass.

Then Middle Billy Goat Gruff
went across the bridge.
Trip-trap, trip-trap,
went his feet.

Out came the ugly troll.
"Who is that, trip-trapping
across my bridge?"
he roared.

"It is I, Middle Billy Goat Gruff,"
said the goat.
"I am coming to gobble you up!"
said the troll.

"Oh, no," said Middle Billy Goat Gruff.
"Wait for my brother,
Big Billy Goat Gruff.
He is much fatter
and tastier than I am."
"All right," said the troll.
"You may cross the bridge."

So Middle Billy Goat Gruff
went into the meadow,
to eat the sweet green grass.

Then Big Billy Goat Gruff
went across the bridge.
He was very big,
and very strong.
TRIP-TRAP, TRIP-TRAP,
went his big, strong feet.

Out came the ugly troll.
"Who is that, TRIP-TRAPPING
across my bridge?"
he roared.

"It is I, Big Billy Goat Gruff," said the goat.

"I am coming to gobble you up!"
said the troll.

"Just see if you can!"
said Big Billy Goat Gruff.

The troll came up onto the bridge.
Big Billy Goat Gruff butted him
with his strong horns.

The troll went flying off the bridge.
He fell into the water
with a loud splash.
He did not come up again.

Big Billy Goat Gruff
went into the meadow,
with his brothers.
They all ate the sweet green grass.

And no one ever saw
the ugly troll again.